Frederick Heathcote Sutton

Church organs

Their position and construction

Frederick Heathcote Sutton

Church organs
Their position and construction

ISBN/EAN: 9783741189166

Manufactured in Europe, USA, Canada, Australia, Japa

Cover: Foto ©Andreas Hilbeck / pixelio.de

Manufactured and distributed by brebook publishing software
(www.brebook.com)

Frederick Heathcote Sutton

Church organs

CHURCH ORGANS:

THEIR POSITION AND CONSTRUCTION.

CHURCH ORGANS:

THEIR POSITION AND CONSTRUCTION.

WITH AN APPENDIX,

CONTAINING SOME ACCOUNT OF THE

MEDIÆVAL ORGAN CASE

STILL EXISTING AT OLD RADNOR, SOUTH WALES.

BY

FREDERICK HEATHCOTE SUTTON, M.A.

VICAR OF THEDDINGWORTH.

RIVINGTONS,

London, Oxford, and Cambridge.

1872.

CHURCH ORGANS:

THEIR POSITION AND CONSTRUCTION.

———•———

THERE is perhaps no article of Church Furniture, not absolutely required for the performance of Divine Service, that receives so much attention as the Organ. Every parish is anxious to become possessed of one; and in these days Organs are a common luxury, even in the smallest and most remote places. Still, with all this anxiety to obtain the best possible instruments (which undoubtedly prevails), it is quite extraordinary how little attention is paid to their appearance; or to the position they ought to occupy.

Churches, in other respects the most gorgeous, are frequently choked up by machines, which are little more than great stacks of pipes; often arranged in such a manner, that no possible ingenuity or expense can ever make them worthy of their position.

In the planning of a Church, the Organ Chamber is now seldom forgotten. But the arrangement of the Organ itself is

B   not

not unfrequently left almost entirely to the Organ Builder, who, naturally enough, considers his object gained, and his responsibilities fulfilled, if the instrument sounds well; forgetting that there is no reason whatever, why an Organ should not sound well, and be made to look very beautiful too.

A great deal has been done in the way of mending matters, by the introduction of the excellent Scudamore Organs for Chancels, which are often designed with great taste, and form a very elegant addition to the furniture of a small Church.

The tendency however, at the present time, seems to be to carry out this principle into very large Organs, and the consequence often is, an instrument which is a complete failure in an architectural point of view. Professional men will be the first to admit, that it is impossible for them to make good designs for Organs, without a thorough knowledge of the mechanism of the Instrument; and will allow, that the true principle to work upon, must be for architects to make themselves thoroughly conversant with the construction of an Organ; and then to ornament the construction to any amount thought desirable; at the same time studying such ancient examples as exist in Europe. It is worth remembering, that a carefully designed Organ will look well, even when money does not allow of its being enclosed in a costly case.

One great difficulty in designing good Gothic Organ Cases, suitable to the beautiful Churches we have learned to build, lies in the extreme rarity of existing examples of mediæval instruments, which we can take as models to work from.

M. Viollet

M. Viollet-Le-Duc gives a short list from France in his "Dictionnaire Raisonné de l'Architecture." There are also a few in Spain, and one certainly in Piedmont (at Sion), while Germany, North and South, with Holland and Belgium, supply a few more, and those perhaps the best and grandest we have ; but when all are enumerated, the number of existing Organs of the Gothic period is extremely small, and the individual specimens are very widely scattered.

The history of the Organ has been so ably and clearly treated by competent writers, during the last few years, that it is quite needless to recapitulate the well-known facts connected with its introduction into Churches.

The object, therefore, of these remarks, will be rather to deal with the present use and arrangement of the Organ, than with its history. As there can be no doubt that (except in very highly-trained choirs) an instrument of some kind is required to keep the voices together, so the public opinion of the present day will no doubt decide, that the Organ is the instrument which should conduct the musical portion of our services. Taking this for granted, the first thing to be settled is, What is the position the Organ should occupy in our churches? As regards the mere sound of the instrument itself, no doubt a place at the west end of a church, or over a choir screen, is by far the best ; for then its tones are able to expand in all directions. But in designing Church Organs, or recommending their position, one has to remember, that the first object in view is not to show off a fine instrument, however grand it may be, but to make that instrument useful in the performance of Divine Service.

The

The object, then, to be aimed at, must be to place the Organ where it can be made to do its work well, and enable the Organist to be near his choir, so as to accompany the singers without difficulty. In old days (now, let us hope, gone for ever) the west-end position was a very good one. The singers were placed in the same gallery with the Organ, and the whole body of sound, from both singers and Organ, was concentrated in one part of the Church; and, however out of place we may think such an arrangement now, very fine musical effects were sometimes produced. But the happy change for the better, which, during the last thirty years, has been coming over our Services, has given a new character to our Church plans and arrangements; and the once usual western gallery, with its Organ, has become a rarity.

Without wishing to restore Organs to their former position, it is almost impossible not to look back with a sort of half regret upon the stately cases, with their rich towers and pilasters, which have succumbed to modern improvements. For instance, it would not be easy to plan a finer architectural effect than the grand old Organ at Finedon Church produces; and let us hope that the increased usefulness of the instrument, has done something to atone for the loss of the sumptuous organcase and gallery, which used to adorn the west end of that magnificent Parish Church, St. Peter's Mancroft, Norwich.

Under present circumstances, the best position for the Organ is, without doubt, at the eastern end of the choir sittings. It would, thus arranged, generally occupy the centre of the chancel wall, north or south, and might project from one to two feet into the chancel, care being taken that the instrument should

should not in any way obstruct the view of the eastern end of
the building; in fact, the less the Organ projects from the wall
the better.

In the accompanying engraving, showing the ground plan
of a Church, the Organ is placed in the position recommended.

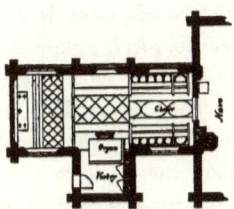

In Wurtemberg, and other parts of Germany, this is a
common situation for the Organ in small Churches, and is found
to answer extremely well, and may safely be recommended as
the most convenient one, and the best suited to our English
choir services. The plan of a Church must of course modify
the arrangement considerably, and, at times, may make it
needful to place the Organ at the east end of an aisle. But
this plan had better not be resorted to unless it is absolutely
necessary, as the Organist is then too far from the singers, who
should always be seated in the chancel if possible. The difficulty of arranging the key-board is one of the great drawbacks
to the present common position of Organs, immediately behind
the choir stalls, in the first bay of a chancel. All sorts of plans
have been tried to find room for the player, and to keep him
out of sight,—which is in itself a mistake,—and in some instances the Organist has been placed even below the singers,
as in a well. This is a great disadvantage, as it prevents his
being able to keep his eye on the choristers and singing men,

so as to secure good order and reverent behaviour in Church. Chancels with aisles of course offer great facilities to the Organ designer, if the arches are of sufficient height.

One word with regard to new Organ chambers. In every case, where it is found necessary to provide an Organ recess, the first care should be to ascertain what sized instrument it is to be built for ; and whether four-feet, eight-feet, or sixteen-feet stops are to be used. The chamber should then be designed amply large enough and as open as possible, and the arch leading into the chancel should be as wide and high as the whole chamber, so as to allow the sound to come out properly. In fact, a kind of shallow transept, with a boarded roof, framed into that of the chancel, would probably be the best form that could be used, thus doing away with the arch altogether.

The engraving has been designed to illustrate the kind of Organ chamber which seems, on the whole, to be the best, while

while its position will be seen to be that which has been recommended on account of its practical convenience.

After having determined where the Organ is to be placed in a Church, the next thing which must occupy the attention of any one wishing to produce a good architectural effect, is the form of the instrument itself, for upon that, in a great measure, must depend the construction of the case with which it is to be clothed.

One of the most important points connected with the construction of Organs, both architecturally and musically, is to get the wind-chest well raised up above the heads of the choristers. If the height of the Church will admit of it, the feet of the pipes should be at least nine or ten feet from the ground, and, if possible, never less than seven feet.

The advantage of this arrangement is, that it allows the sound to travel over the heads of the singers, and makes the instrument much pleasanter to sing to. The effect in the body of the Church is better, and it gives the architect a chance of throwing something like dignity into the design for the Organ-case, enabling him to make it group effectively with the screens, stalls, and other furniture of the chancel.

There are, of course, numberless instances where lack of funds will prevent an architect from suggesting a rich Organ-case; but a carefully-designed and well-arranged instrument will never look out of place, even if it be made of the plainest materials. Besides, a well-designed Organ can be enriched at any time, and its case completed as money comes in.

The

The lofty Churches on the Continent enabled the old architects and Organ builders to place their Organs, if they thought well, at a very considerable elevation above the floor, and many beautiful Gothic Organ-lofts are still left, though, except in comparatively few instances, the Organs have disappeared. In our larger English Churches no doubt the same arrangement was common; indeed, the carved heads, which used to support the Organ, still exist on the south side of the nave at Wells Cathedral, and the original bosses for the brackets of the Organ gallery are yet to be seen on the east side of the south transept of Christ Church Cathedral, Oxford.

The Organ at old St. Paul's, which seems from the views to have been Gothic, stood over the stalls on the north side of the choir, but still well elevated above the singers.

In the general run of our Churches, however, there is neither width for the necessary projection of the gallery, nor sufficient height to allow the Organs to be arranged in the foreign manner, so that we must be content, for the most part, to place them nearer the ground.

In constructing a Gothic, or indeed any style of Organ, all the different parts should be made to show themselves well. This was almost invariably the case in old instances, though the rule is not universal, as the Organ at Gonesse, near Paris (dated 1508), has a moulding below the pipes, instead of showing the wind-chest. It has, however, an awkward look, even in that very picturesque instrument.

By way of illustration, let us suppose an Organ to be required for a fair-sized Church, where there is a well-constructed
Organ-chamber,

Organ-chamber, the full height of the chancel walls. The lower part of the recess would probably be required as a vestry for the Clergy and choir, for which purpose it would answer admirably. This chamber would most likely be floored, about eight or nine feet above the ground, so as to allow height enough in the vestry; and the space above the floor would be a chamber opening into the chancel, say from sixteen to eighteen feet high. In this chamber there would be ample room for a very fine instrument, sufficient for the requirements of any Church short of cathedral scale and dignity.

The engraving shows the construction of an Organ designed

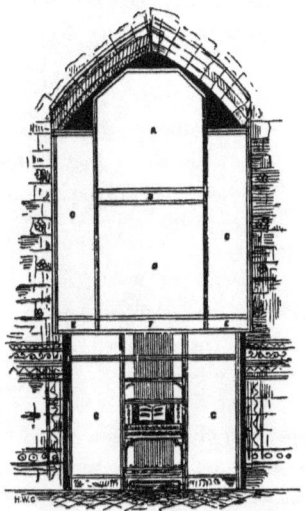

(A) Swell Organ. (B) Wind Chest to Swell. (C) Pedal Organ. (D) Great Organ.
(E) Pedal Wind Chest. (F) Wind Chest. (G) Space for action.

D   to suit

to suit such a position. It might contain from twelve to twenty stops, or thereabouts. The sketch will at once explain the arrangement.

In this case the Organ-chamber would supply room for the bellows as well as for the other parts of the instrument; and it should be remembered that no well-built Organ ought ever to require the bellows to be kept constantly working, even when the full chorus is in use, as they should always be made large enough to supply any wind that may be required, without difficulty.

It will be seen here that the great organ is placed immediately over the organist, while above that is the swell organ. On each side of the instrument the pedal pipes are arranged on two wind chests.

This plan is a very useful one, as it secures the pedal pipes being distinctly heard in the Church,—a very important thing, —particularly when Bourdons are used instead of the more powerful open sixteen-feet pipes.

In this stage the plan of the Organ would be ready to be placed in the hands of the architect to receive its ornamental woodwork; though he would, of course, have arranged the form of the instrument previously, and the curves of the pipes, so as to suit the requirements of the Church for which he was designing.

The details of the case should be made to harmonize in style with the rest of the fittings of the chancel, so that the whole might form one well-considered scheme of architectural decoration.

In

In still larger instruments the same principle has only to be applied to insure a fine effect. In Churches where want of room, or any other cause, makes it necessary that the Organ should be placed against the wall of the chancel itself, some modification of the well-known "Scudamore Organs" would generally be found satisfactory, care being taken to allow sufficient space to admit of the bellows being large enough to secure a thoroughly good and steady supply of wind.

Where an Organ is intended to hang over at the sides in the usual mediæval manner, and when room cannot be obtained behind, it will be found a good arrangement to allow the lower part of the case containing the bellows to project a little on each side also.

A small Organ constructed on this plan, suitable for a village Church, is shown in the accompanying engraving.

When the architect does not intend using the common Gothic form alluded to, this plan of gaining extra bellows-room need not be adopted, as the base of the Organ would usually, under such circumstances, supply all the space required.

In order to illustrate this subject more fully, and give a general idea of the kind of arrangement recommended for the cases of Church Organs, several designs have been given— which, it is hoped, will be found useful to those who are anxious to impart a dignified and architectural character to the fine instruments which have become of late almost a necessity in our churches.

Figure 1 will explain the first process in making a design for an Organ Case, as it shows the construction of the instrument. The design is that of a Chancel Organ, suited to a small Church, and is arranged so as to stand against the wall at the East end of the Choir Sittings.   It might contain from 3 to 6 stops conveniently.

Figure 2 shows the same Organ with the pipes arranged in three compartments ; the three centre pipes rising so as to form a kind of tower.   Here the lower part of the Organ is cased in, the position of the bellows and wind chest being still clearly marked out by the framing.

Figure 3 shows the same Organ, further cased and decorated; the same construction however being still preserved. Here ornament is added by means of rich open-work pipe-shades, and a cresting above the upper moulding. The front has shutters adapted to it, which increase the picturesque effect very much
                                                            where

where there is space for them. This is often a convenient and useful arrangement, as the shutters can be closed during the cleaning of a Church; and thus a great deal of dust and dirt may be kept out of the Organ.

In a Gothic Organ, the arrangement of the front pipes, as a rule, shows the disposition of the pipes in all the different stops contained in the instrument.

Figure 4 is a view of the Organ originally built for Bilton Church, near Rugby. It is a rather larger instrument than the last, and is constructed on the same plan, but shows the wind chest extended beyond the lower part of the case, and supported by brackets on either side. This very usual Gothic arrangement (shown also in the Old Radnor Organ) gives greater space for arranging the pipes, without making the lower parts of the Organ case, inconveniently large and cumbersome. In this Organ also, the upper part is framed into three compartments, the pipes rising in one sweep from the sides to the centre. The pipe-shades are handsomely carved with an open-work pattern of foliage, and follow in their form the natural curve taken by the pipes. The Organ is surmounted by a deep cresting, and the whole case is painted and gilt, the ground colour being a dark chocolate, upon which are stencilled Gothic patterns. The shutters, in this instance, are elaborately stencilled with a scroll pattern, on a blue ground, and are enriched with medallions containing angels playing on musical instruments; painted on a gold ground.

No. 5 shows the side view of the same Organ, with the shutters partly closed.

E   Figures

Figures 6, 7, 8 form another group of Organs, in which the bellows are placed in a separate chamber. This is a very convenient plan, and gives ample space for larger instruments than those hitherto described. Organs occupying this position, can be furnished with a key-board either behind or at the side of the instrument; if it be found more convenient, and if desired, a tracker action can be used, and the manuals placed below, so as to allow the organist to play from one of the stalls.

Figure 9 is an Organ of the same class, but suitable to a larger church, where an instrument of 15 or 20 stops is required. It is designed for two manuals.

Figure 10 represents a grand Organ, for a Cathedral, or very large Church where there is a triforium. The triforium in this case would contain the bellows very conveniently. This Organ is designed without the usual Gothic folding shutters, as from their enormous size they would be an inconvenience rather than an advantage. Some of the largest mediæval instruments however, which have come down to us, were fitted originally with these immense painted wings, while several of the smaller Gothic Organs still retain them.

Figures 11, 12, 13, and 14 have been drawn to show that the fine old Organs of the 18th century are by no means so difficult to convert into Organs suitable to a Gothic Church, as is frequently supposed. They are often very fine instruments, and a little Gothic detail carefully arranged would frequently make them into Organs of great beauty.

Figure 11 shows an Organ of this class.

Figure

Figure 12 shows the same organ in its Gothic dress, but unaltered in its plan and arrangement.

Figure 13 shows a still more commonplace instrument.

Figure 14 shows the same Organ with its pipes re-arranged, and decorated with carving and stencilling.

Figure 15 is a small Chamber or Chancel Organ, designed with early English detail.

Figure 16 is an organ designed for three manuals, and suitable to a large parish Church.

In this instrument, the choir organ is placed immediately over the key-board, and is shown with its own shutters open.

It would be found a very convenient arrangement, if a small pair of separate bellows were provided for the supply of wind to the choir organ in this instance, as it could then be blown by one of the choir boys, without difficulty, when the full power of the instrument was not wanted, which it seldom would be, for the ordinary daily services.

This extra pair of bellows might be disconnected; when the large bellows for supplying the full organ were in use, which should be made large enough for the whole instrument.

It seems most probable that the Organs in large Churches, especially in England, were frequently placed, in Gothic times, on the Rood screens, where we still find them in many of our
Cathedrals

Cathedrals and Minsters ; and that the Organs so commonly set up on the Rood lofts, at the Restoration, only replaced similar instruments ; which had been destroyed, or become out of repair.

In accordance with this idea, a suggestive drawing (fig. 17) has been added in the present edition of this work, showing an Organ placed on a screen.

In this design the Organ case terminates in a large floriated cross, which may not impossibly have been the way in which the cross and Organ case were combined ; in Churches where the Organ occupied the central position, and where no separate beam existed to carry the cross itself.

The well-known Organ in Notre Dame at Bruges suggests that some such arrangement may not have been uncommon ; though the Organ there is a small one, and seems rather to group itself round the foot of the cross, than the cross to form part of the Organ case. The Bruges Organ is a late one, though the cross is Gothic. The effect however, on the whole is picturesque and good.

Design No. 17 is not intended for a very large instrument, but for an Organ suitable to a good-sized Parish Church. But there would be, of course, but little difficulty in arranging one for a Cathedral if required. In larger instruments it would probably be necessary sometimes, to place the pedal Organ in the triforium, especially if thirty-two feet pipes were used.

The position on the screen, however, can only be recommended

mended in special cases, and in churches where there is plenty of height and space at command.

The writer notices with great pleasure the increased attention which some of the first Architects of the day are giving to the Organ-cases they have to deal with. The new one at St. Mary's at Nottingham, designed by Mr. Scott, should be especially mentioned. It is in many respects admirable, though it suffers greatly from the narrowness of the chancel in which it is placed. If it stood under the tower arches of that fine Church, either north or south, the beauty of its design would at once be apparent, while its musical effect would be greatly increased.

In the Appendix will be found the drawings of the Old Radnor Organ-case; as well as some sketches of the elegant, but little-known Organ at Framlingham Church, Suffolk.

There are, however, many old Organs in England which well deserve attention—the writer has therefore placed in the Appendix a short list of Organs which seem particularly worthy of study, on account of their form and construction.

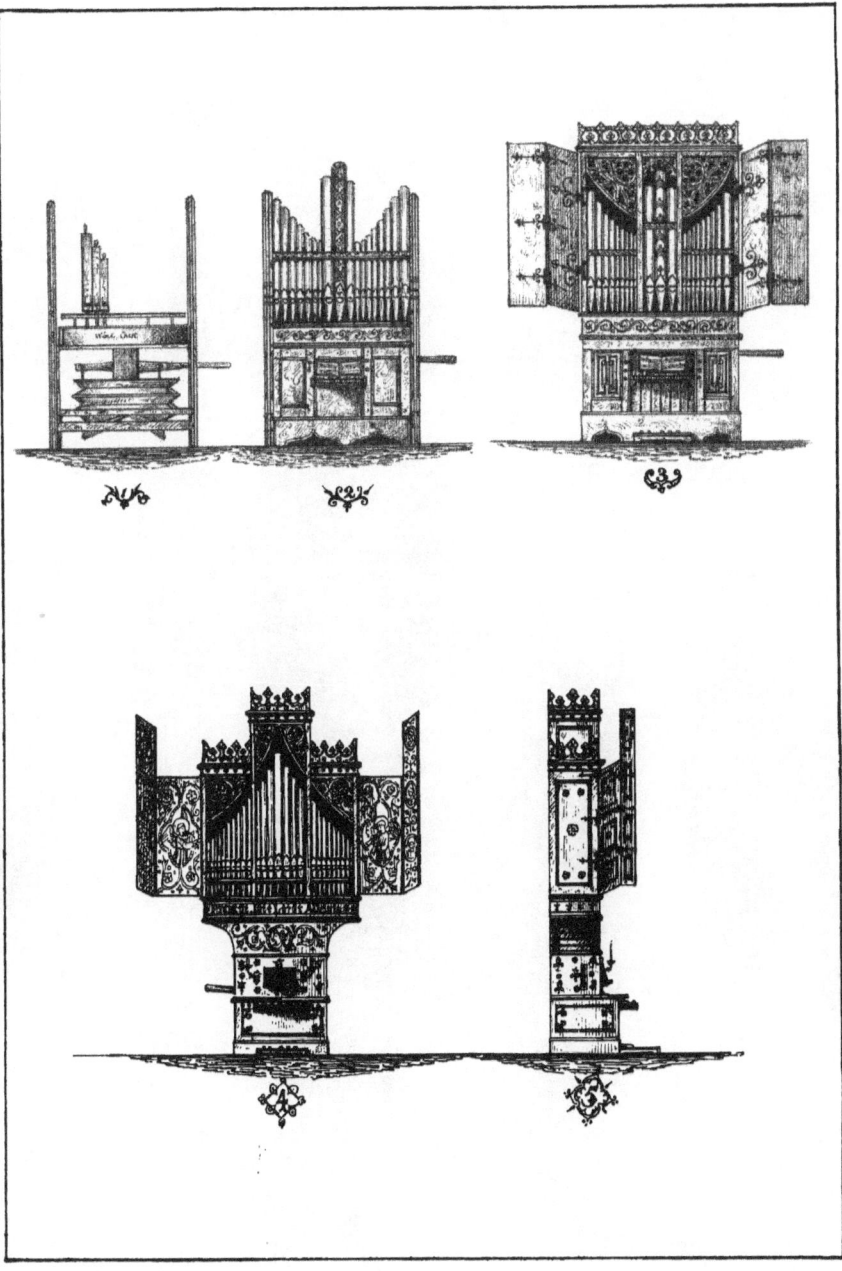

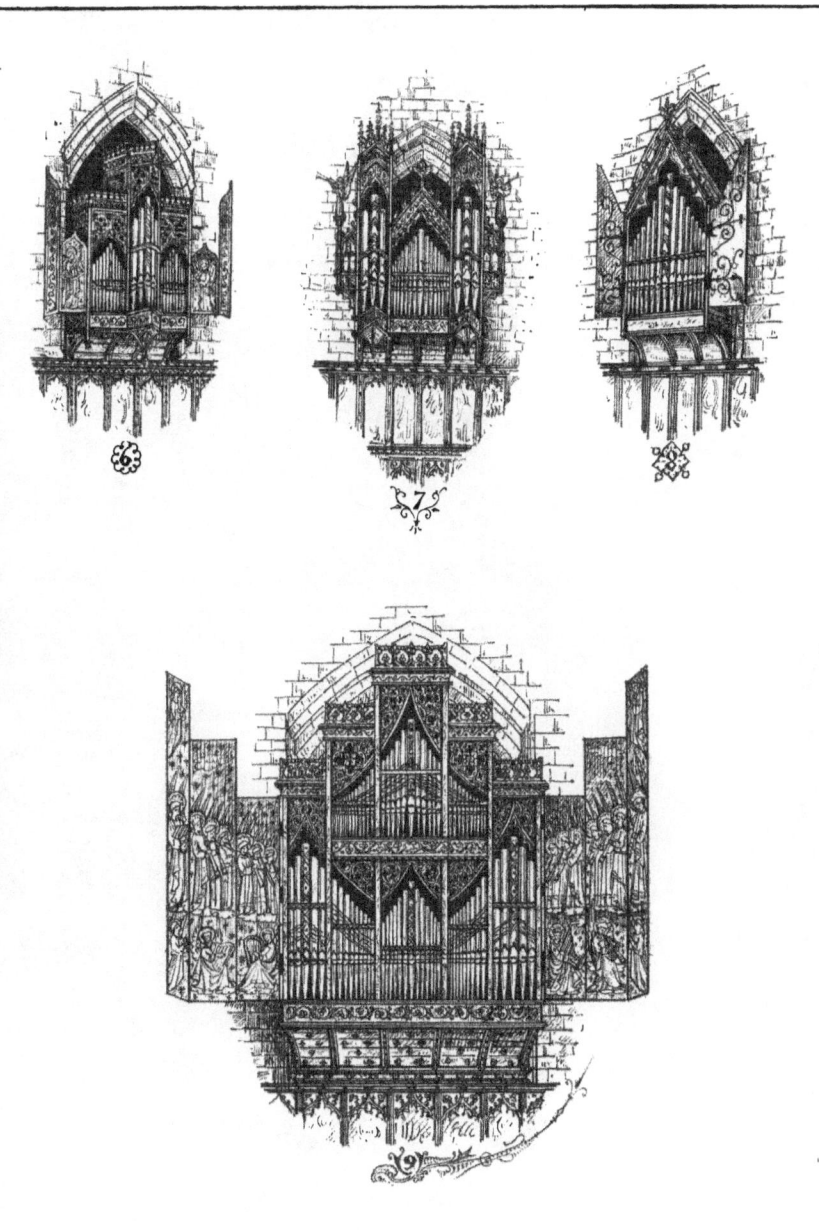

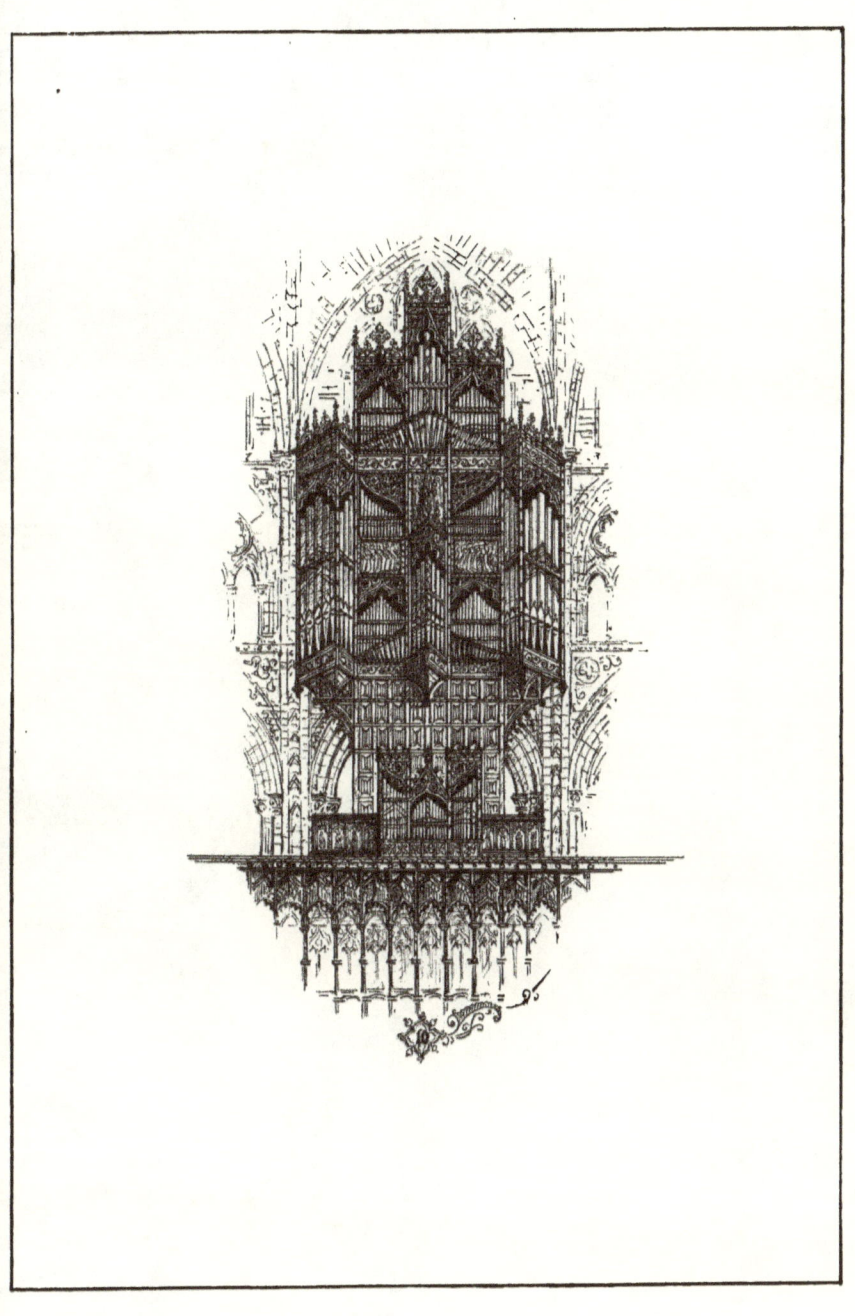

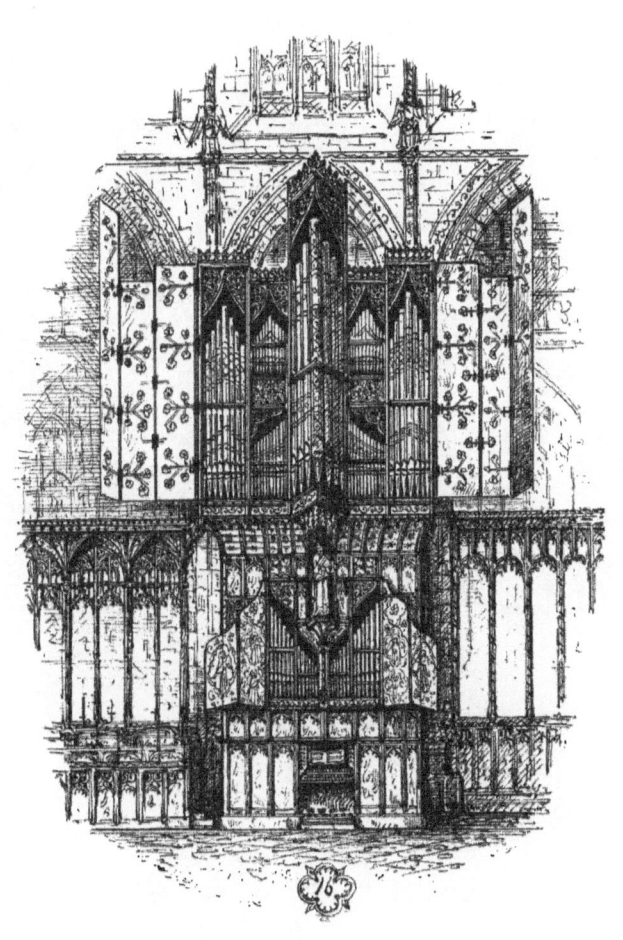

APPENDIX.

APPENDIX.

IN the present edition of this work, the short account of the Gothic Organ-case at Old Radnor, in South Wales, has been retained in the Appendix, in order that the foregoing remarks may be illustrated by the earliest example of an English Organ at present known to exist.

The dimensions of the Old Radnor Organ-case, which is of oak, and elaborately carved and panelled, are as follows :—

	FEET.	INCHES.
Total height	18	0
Width above wind chest . . .	9	4
Width below wind chest . . .	5	9
Height up to hang-over . . .	5	10
Height of cresting and pinnacles .	1	8
Depth of the Organ . . .	2	6

As will be seen from the accompanying views, the front is divided into five compartments, three of which are occupied by the larger pipes, standing in projecting towers (Figure 1), while

G   the

the intervening spaces are flat, and contain two tiers of small
pipes, each compartment being divided midway by a square
panel of rich carved work.

The rest of the case is almost entirely covered by napkin-
pattern panels of the best description and of very intricate
design (Figure 5); the whole composition being finished at the
top of the Organ with a deep cresting of pinnacles and semi-
circles, upon which are seated grotesque animals.

This cresting, though debased in style, compared with much
of the detail in other parts of the case, has a very rich effect,
and when painted and gilded, as no doubt it once was, must
have looked extremely well.

Below the key-board, the panels are plain, with the exception
of the three central ones in the front, these are perforated with
a number of openings of different forms (Figure 1). The
central panel and that on the right hand have very elegant
openings of Gothic tracery, the larger ones being formed of
double triangles interlaced. These were no doubt intended to
let out the sound of the choir organ.

This position for the choir organ was not uncommon in old
Organs, specimens exist at Moret, near Paris, and in the small
Organ in the nave of the Cathedral at Metz. The two holes in
the left hand panel below the key-board (Figure 1) probably
show that at Old Radnor the choir organ consisted of two stops
only.

There is an excellent arrangement at the back of the
instrument,

instrument, which would always be useful in cased Organs.
This consists of large folding shutters, which open, so as to
allow the pipes to be tuned, and any needful repairs to be
done, without taking any part of the case to pieces.   It is
hardly necessary to remind the reader what a great advantage
such an arrangement must be ; for any one who has seen an
Organ tuned, must have noticed what a troublesome process
it often is : the difficulty of getting at the pipes being frequently an almost insuperable obstacle to putting them properly
in tune.

There is also another arrangement, in the plan of this
Organ, which might be adopted where needful and possible,
with great advantage, by which ample space is secured for the
bellows.   For this purpose the lower part of the Organ is made
to project into the aisle, at the back of the instrument, two or
three feet.   This allows of any room that may be required for
the lungs of the Organ, without in any way spoiling its appearance in the Chancel of the Church.   (Figure 2.)

The writer has great pleasure in stating that during the
last few months, the Old Radnor Organ-case has been most
carefully and beautifully repaired—every detail having received
the greatest attention—and that a new Organ is at once to be
fitted into it, arranged expressly to suit it ; in order that the old
wood-work may not be in any way cut about or interfered with.
When completed, the Organ will be replaced in its old position;
once more to lead the music in the Church, where it has stood
so long, silently waiting for better days.

In order to illustrate the subject still further ; a few drawings

ings have been added, of another very remarkable and little known Organ, *i. e.* that still in use at Framlingham Church, Suffolk. (Figure 7.)

This instrument is apparently of about the time of Henry VIII., and is said to have been originally placed, like the Old Radnor Organ, in front of one of the arches of the choir; a tradition which is confirmed by the construction of the Organ itself, the towers of which are cut away at the back, so as to fit partly under an arch.

The details of this Organ-case are very elegant and beautiful, and are extremely well executed. The open-work carving of the little screen, which conceals the player (Figure 8), deserves especial notice from the elegance of its design.

Figure 9 represents one of the panels on either side of the key-board; it is carved so as to represent a groined interior, and produces rather a rich effect.

The front pipes appear to be all original, and are covered with a handsome diaper. The mouth of one of the large pipes (Figure 10) has been drawn, to show the peculiar form adopted. It will be seen that the lower part is trefoiled, which gives it a very Gothic look. The instrument itself, appears to be principally the work of Snetzler; but it has been much altered since his time. It is still, however, a good Organ, as far as it goes.

It is to be hoped that this picturesque old Organ may some day find its way back to its original position in the choir of the
Church,

Church, where it would look much better than it does now, in the western gallery, for which it was seemingly never designed.

The writer very much regrets that he is unable to give illustrations of the beautiful little Organ at Stanford Church, Leicestershire. Though apparently a little later than the one at Framlingham, it is well worthy of study, especially on account of its pipes, which are ornamented with patterns hammered in the metal, and look remarkably well.

The following short list of old Organs will be found useful to any one anxious to study the subject; they are of various dates, but all more or less interesting and instructive :—

(1) Framlingham Church, Suffolk.
(2) King's College Chapel, Cambridge.
(3) Tewkesbury Abbey Church.
(4) St. John's College, Cambridge.   (Old Organ.)
(5) Stanford Church, Leicestershire.
(6) Worcester Cathedral.
(7) Gloucester Cathedral.
(8) Rugby Church.
(9) St. Paul's Cathedral.
(10) Southwell Minster.
(11) Finedon Church, Northants.
(12) Norwich Cathedral.

Many others might of course be mentioned of almost equal interest. Indeed, scattered up and down this country, numbers of old Organs still exist which give us all the information which

H   we

we require to enable us to design good Organ-cases, and which have as yet received much less attention than they deserve.

Each year, of course, sees the number shortened, as Church after Church comes under the hands of the restorer; but there are still enough left to teach us almost all we need know as far as Organ-building is concerned, of the craft of our forefathers.

FINIS.

GILBERT AND RIVINGTON, PRINTERS, ST. JOHN'S SQUARE, LONDON.

Gothic Organ Case Old Radnor Ch.
S.ᵗ Wales

(1)

The Choir Old Radnor Ch. Restored.

(N 2. B)

Eastern End of Organ Case
Restored.

(N 2. A)

Nº 2
East end of the Radnor Organ

No 3.

Part of tracery
over pulpit. East Tower.

Tracing over the
Lower row of 13. small
Pipes.

(N 4.)

(N 5)

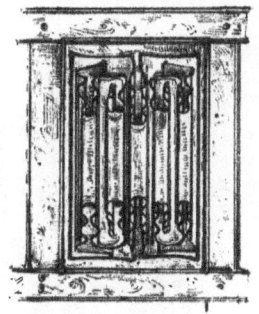

Linen Pattern. Panel. over.
the Radar.

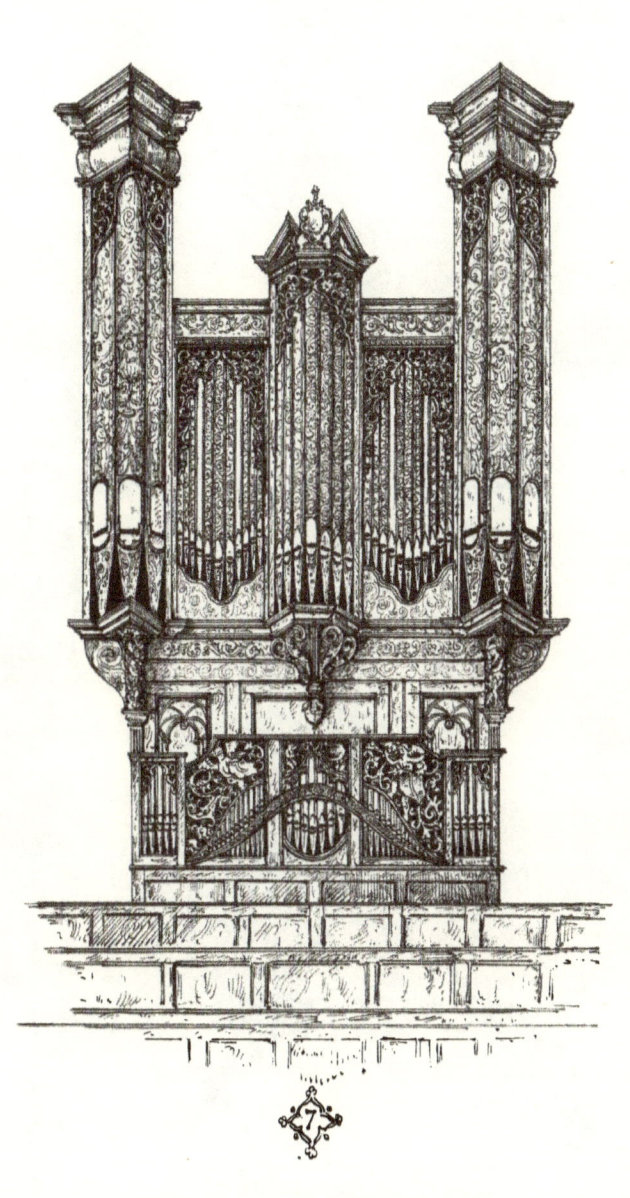

www.ingramcontent.com/pod-product-compliance
Lightning Source LLC
Chambersburg PA
CBHW021231260626
47172CB00002B/716